With love to all my family, especially Madeleine,
and with many thanks to Paul Dowswell –L.A.

For my brother Steven, with love
Thanks go to my friends at the Lion & Unicorn,
The Pavilion, and the lovely people at Scholastic –S.H.

tiger tales
an imprint of ME Media, LLC
202 Old Ridgefield Road, Wilton, CT 06897
Published in the United States 2010
Originally published in Great Britain 2008
by Scholastic Children's Books
a division of Scholastic Ltd.
Text copyright © 2008 Laura Adkins
Illustrations copyright © 2008 Sam Hearn
CIP data is available
Printed in Singapore
TWP0110
Hardcover ISBN-13: 978-1-58925-085-7
Hardcover ISBN-10: 1-58925-085-0
Paperback ISBN-13: 978-1-58925-418-3
Paperback ISBN-10: 1-58925-418-X

Ordinary Oscar

by Laura Adkins   *Illustrated by* Sam Hearn

tiger tales

In the moonlit garden of 16 Slug Street,
the snails are busy.
Slowly, they munch and crunch
the tasty, tender leaves of potted plants
and juicy lettuce.
They are all happy snails.

Well, **nearly**
all of them….

Oscar Slimeglider
was **not** happy.
"I'm **tired** of sleeping
all day," he said.

"I'm **fed up** with
eating all night.

"I'm bored with being greenish-grayish-brownish.

"I want other snails to look at me and say, 'Wow! There's Oscar Slimeglider!'

I want to be different....

"Nonsense!" said Oscar's dad.
"What's wrong with sleeping all day?
What's wrong with eating all night?"

"And what's wrong with being
greenish-grayish-brownish?" said
Oscar's mom. "Your twenty-five brothers and
sisters never complain."

"We never complain!"

But Oscar was **determined.**

"The Wise Old Snail will know what to do," he declared.

So off he went.

"What do you want
to be famous **for**?" asked
the Wise Old Snail.

"Can you paint?

Dance?

Play the guitar?"

Oscar shook his head.

"Being famous isn't **always** easy, you know,"
said the Wise Old Snail. "Are you **sure** about this?"

Oscar nodded.

"Very well then," said the Wise Old Snail. "You're
going to need a bit of **magic**."

And he told Oscar what to do.

Oscar waited patiently for the sun to rise.

Then he **turned** around three times and cried,

"Slime, slime! Slither, slither!

Fairy Godsnail, please come hither!"

The **Fairy Godsnail** appeared.
"So you want to be famous?" she asked.

Oscar wiggled eagerly. "Yes, please!"

"There's only one thing to do then," replied the **Fairy Godsnail**. "I shall grant you three wishes. But choose carefully," she warned.

Then she waved her **magic wand** and disappeared.

Oscar closed his eyes tightly and made a **wish**....

Slowly, Oscar opened his eyes.
"Look at me!" he gasped.

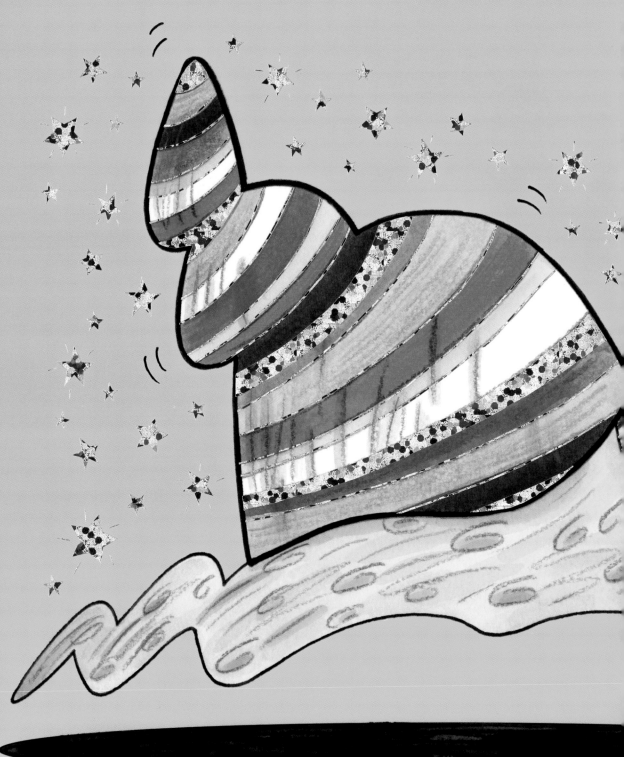

"I'll be famous for being the most marvelous mollusk!

I'm a stunning, stupendous, spectacular snail! Everyone will admire me."

And sure enough, someone was admiring Oscar....

Up above, a **hungry** bird
smiled to himself.

"That snail looks like a
terrifically tasty treat,"
he thought, plunging down.

"Get your great **greedy**
beak **off** me!" Oscar wailed.

"I wish I was
bigger than you…

"much...

"much...

"BIGGER!"

Oscar landed in town. He was bigger than a bus, bigger than six buses glued together.

As the sun began to sink, Oscar slithered into the woods to **hide**.

"Now I'm famous for being frightening," he said, "and I have no **friends**."

Oscar began to **cry**.

"I want to go **home**
to Mom and Dad and my
twenty-five brothers and
sisters. I wish I was just
ordinary Oscar again."

And just like that…

he was home.

"Where have you been, Oscar?" asked his dad. "We've been awfully worried about you."

"We thought you might have been squashed!" said his mom.

"Now, it's dinnertime," she said. "I've got some tasty, tender leaves, just for you."

"Mmm, my favorite," said Oscar. "Maybe being ordinary isn't so bad after all."

B ut sometimes,
just sometimes, even an
ordinary snail can do
extraordinary things.

S ix weeks later…

THAT'S MY BOY!

By **Mike Mollusk**
Garden Correspondent

Shellebrity: Oscar Slimeglider rescues Mom trapped in shifting soil

CONTEST: Win a copy of *G*

Snail

When Mrs. Gertrude Slimeglider fell into some shifting soil, she was overcome by panic.

Gertrude, who is expecting sixty eggs next week, was trapped.

Meanwhile, her twenty-six children—Agnes, Bernard, Cornelius, Destiny, Electra, Fifi, Georgina, Heathcliff, Ingrid, Jethro, Keanu, Lavender, Mozart, Norbert, Oscar, Pandora, Quentin, Rupert, Sigmund, Thomas, Ursula, Veronica, Wilma, Xavier, Yeats, and Zebedee—roamed the flower bed.

"I told Agnes to get her dad, but because he was so far away I knew that would take a long time," she said.

With her husband on the other side of the garden, Gertrude was desperate, until clever Oscar came to the rescue.

"Oscar is a brave and caring snail."

Oscar, a Saint Mollusk pupil, gathered his siblings together. Under his direction, they began to eat the surrounding plants. The courageous youngster kept his cool and soon the soil began to shift, allowing Gertrude to escape.

"Oscar is a brave and caring snail. I'm really proud of him," said Gertrude. "When my husband gets home and hears about what happened, I know he'll be proud, too."